Romeo
AND Juliet
TOGETHER
(and ALIVE!)
AT LAST

**A
Richard
Jackson
Book**

Romeo AND Juliet

TOGETHER (and ALIVE!) AT LAST

AVI

ORCHARD BOOKS · NEW YORK

Orchard Books
95 Madison Avenue
New York, New York 10016

J.
Avi
Gift 9/02

Replacement copy

Manufactured in the United States of America
Book design by Mina Greenstein
10
The text of this book is set in 12 pt. Times.

Library of Congress Cataloging-in-Publication Data
Avi, 1937-   Romeo and Juliet—together (and alive!) at last.
Summary: The eighth grade's plan to get two reluctant
"lovers" together by means of a classroom production of
Shakespeare's play has some very unexpected results.
[1. Schools—Fiction. 2. Plays—Fiction. 3. Friend-
ship—Fiction. 4. Humorous stories] I. Title.
PZ7.A953Ro   1987   [Fic]   87-7680
ISBN 0-531-05721-6
ISBN 0-531-08321-7 (lib. bdg.)

FOR SALTZ, the real Saltz.
And my oldest friend.

1

PETE SALTZ and I have been best friends for as long as I can remember. At South Orange River Middle School, eighth grade, we sit, eat lunch, and do weekends together. If I'm not at his house, he's at mine. Close as a pair of crossed eyes. There isn't much I don't know about him. At least that's what I thought.

Turned out Saltz had a secret.

One nice warm spring day we were heading home from school, and Saltz wasn't saying much. Normally, he has the fastest mouth this side of Nervous Purvis, a local radio DJ we like to hear. And I had been talking about Albert Hamilton.

Hamilton is the worst kind of bully: he's great at almost everything—grades, sports, and if the girls tell me true, looks. People wouldn't mind except Hamilton makes sure you know it. The way he sees it, he's God's gift to himself.

As far as I know he has only one flaw: the guy is

a pyromaniac. Fire fascinates him. Give him a barn fire, a matchbook, a firecracker, and he's in a world of his own.

I was talking about Hamilton's attempts to build bigger, better firecrackers in science lab when I realized Saltz hadn't said anything for five minutes. Then, when we reached his place, he just said, "See ya," and drifted toward his front door.

"Hey!" I called, only then sensing that things weren't right. "What's up? You mad at me?"

Saltz stopped. "You wouldn't understand," he said.

"What wouldn't I understand?"

"Nothing."

"How can I not understand nothing? Do *you* understand?"

"No," he admitted.

"How about giving me a try," I coaxed. His hand was on the doorknob.

"It's just . . ." His voice trailed off.

"Hey, I'm your best friend, remember?"

After a moment he let go of the door. But he didn't say anything; he just sat down on his front steps.

"What," he said, "do you think of Anabell Stackpoole?"

"Stackpoole?" I said, surprised. She's a girl in our class.

2

"Yeah," he said, "Anabell Stackpoole." His facial expression reminded me of how my dog looks when we're about to go off for a day at the beach and he knows he's staying home.

"What about her?" I said.

"I . . . I like her."

"Since when?"

He thought hard. "Two days ago."

"What happened then?"

He shrugged. "Just . . . happened."

"She like you?"

He shook his head. "She doesn't even notice me."

"You try talking to her?"

Now his look suggested how stupid I was.

"Want *me* to talk to her?"

Panic crept into his eyes.

"Okay. What are you going to do about it?"

He struggled for an answer. What he came up with was "I wrote a poem about her."

I wasn't surprised. Saltz was our poet, a kind of local Shakespeare. "Can I see it?" I asked.

From out of his portable bag of junk he hauled a spiral notebook. The spiral was half off, like a worm desperately seeking air.

Finding a sheet of ruled paper with words set between the wrinkles, he handed it over. This is what he had written:

3

ANABELL

There once was a fair beauty named Anabell
For whom Pete Saltz, truly, in love fell.
But when he offered his heart,
She jumped up with a start,
And said, "I have to go now because I just
heard the end-of-the-class-bell."

I looked from Saltz to the poem, then back to
him, until it fully hit me: Saltz was in love!

NORMALLY, Saltz traveled to school like a blind blimp. A blimp that's still trailing its mooring ropes. And his idea of getting anyplace—class, dinner, a movie, anywhere—is to arrive a half hour late.

But the morning after I had learned his secret, not only were his shirttails tucked in, but his shoelaces were tied. Or anyway, at least one shoe was tied. And we actually got to class early. Not even Mrs. Misakian, our homeroom teacher, was there.

Saltz, who hadn't mentioned Stackpoole once, went right to his desk, took out paper and pencil, and began writing.

"Homework?" I asked.

His stare clearly said: "Mind your own business!" And he hunched over his paper and began to chew his pencil. But whenever someone came into the room, he looked up. I got it: he was watching for Stackpoole.

She came, appearing in the doorway like an almost extinct breed of mouse about to attend a convention of cats. At the threshold she paused. It didn't seem to me she noticed Saltz at all. But when Saltz saw her he blotched red, ducked over his work, and began scribbling like crazy. The fact that he refused to look at her again told me tons.

Stackpoole, meanwhile, went right to her corner seat, which was way back and off to one side, by the class gerbil. I couldn't hear her steps on the floor.

Stackpoole's voice, which she didn't use often, was hardly more than a whisper. Her legs and arms were thin, her hands small. A narrow, freckled face was partially hidden behind stringy brown hair, which she sucked on. Maybe it was her only nourishment. If she wasn't eating this hair, she was brushing it out of her eyes to see the book she was always reading.

Sure enough, once in her seat she got out a paperback, drew up her knees, caught her heels on the edge of her chair, and began to read. I mean, she dove into that book. First she'd read a page, then she'd flick the hair out of her face, then a page, then her hair . . . so it went.

The classroom began to fill. More and more racket and horsing around. But there they were: Saltz on one side of the room, Stackpoole on the other, as if each was at the opposite side of the *world*.

I gave Saltz a nudge. "Hey," I whispered. "She's here."

"What?" he grunted, still writing.

"Stackpoole," I said, speaking softly.

He offered a frown.

"She's sitting there—" I pointed her out—"just reading."

That time he ignored me completely.

"If you like her so much, why don't you talk to her?"

"Busy," he mumbled, his face looking like the skin of a radish. I tried to see what he was writing, but he slapped an elbow over his work.

I decided to check her out myself.

First I went to the back of the room, pretending to study the gerbil. Then I hunkered down by the rack of award-winning paperback books we have for silent reading and looked at the cover of her book. It had a picture of a woman trying to get her clothes either on or off, hard to tell which. They were old-fashioned clothes, too, something like a founding mother might have worn. Also, there was a founding father standing around, obviously embarrassed by the whole thing. I guess he was supposed to be at Bunker Hill. The book was called *Passion's Revolt.*

"Newbery winner?" I asked.

Pushing the hair away from her eyes, Stackpoole pulled her freckled face out of her book. "What?" she said, her voice a whisper.

7

"That book—it any good?"

"Yes."

"What's it about?"

"History."

I glanced over at Saltz. He was ignoring us, but I was sure he knew where I was.

"You read a lot, don't you?" I said to Stackpoole.

"Yes."

"So does Saltz," I offered, waiting to see if she would react. A vague flicker of something buried deep did come through, though she herself couldn't have been taller than four feet six.

She went back to her reading.

I stood up, puzzled, trying to figure out what to do. I was pretty sure that these two were in love. But then, when I stopped and thought about it, I realized something. I didn't really know what *love* was.

3

"LOVE."

I had heard a lot about it on TV, in songs, even in notes passed around in class. I never took it personally. Sure, Hays's kid sister had a crush on me. That didn't count. Love, real love, was something that happened to other people. Older people. Now I had to deal with it.

In the back of our classroom is a huge dictionary. I went right there and looked up the word *love*. The definition read:

> The attraction, desire, or affection felt for a person who arouses delight, or admiration, or elicits tenderness, sympathetic interest, or benevolence; devoted affection (a mother's —— for her child).

I was staggered. For the first time in my life I understood how hard it must be to be in love. Those things—all of them—had to be done and all at the same time! No wonder I had never been in love. I didn't even know what all those words meant.

Good thing I was going to school.

I looked up the biggies, like "sympathetic interest," and "elicits tenderness" (which sounded kinky). Obviously, love took a whole lot of energy, not to mention guts.

All the same, I felt a whole new sympathy for people in love. And more. After all, a best friend is someone you help when things go bad. And here was Saltz, *my* best friend, sunk in a pit of sympathetic interest.

He needed help.

During midmorning recess I met with my other buddies—Hays, who had a mohawk haircut that month, and Radosh, who loved class politics—to clue them in to what was happening. As we talked, we munched our snacks.

"You're not going to believe this," I announced when I had cleared my throat of doughnut holes. "Saltz is in love."

They looked at me as if I had spoken a foreign language.

"Seriously," I said, "it's true. Saltz is in love. Really."

"With someone?" asked Hays.

I nodded. "Anabell Stackpoole. Not only is Saltz in love with her," I continued, "I think he has an attraction, desire, or affection for her, too. And while

10

I know it's hard to believe, she seems to be arousing delight, admiration, tenderness (of an elicit kind), sympathetic interest, as well as benevolence and devoted affection. Not to mention a mother's blank space for her child."

"I thought you said he was in love," said Hays.

"That is love," I said. To prove it I showed them the dictionary definition I had copied and memorized.

Hays read it carefully, then looked up. "That's not what they show on 'Dallas,'" he said.

"Or 'Miami Vice,'" agreed Radosh, who was reading over Hays's shoulder.

We talked, voices hushed. The situation was new. As far as we knew, Saltz was the first boy in our class to fall in love.

We looked across the field at him. He was hitching up his trousers and shoving peanut butter cookies into his mouth.

We gazed past him to the other side of the field. There was Stackpoole, sitting under a tree and reading, looking more like a rejected acorn than anything.

"You know," said Hays, "they don't look like they're in love."

"Saltz is," I assured them.

"Yeah, Sitrow," Radosh added, "but what makes you so sure about Stackpoole?"

I had to admit I wasn't sure.

"Don't you think you should find out?" Hays suggested.

MOST PEOPLE my age look like bargain basement rejects. Lucy Neblet, who is in our class, can pass (at top speed) for fifteen. She's what we pray our futures will look like, a living hope that we'll get to look older and better, maybe even make the cover of *People* magazine. The word is she even dates guys from tenth grade.

Crispy, sharp-edged Lucy's fingernails are painted, her lipstick is bright, her hair is never mussed. The one girl in class to carry a hair dryer in her lunch box, Lucy not only thinks she's the prettiest girl in class, she is.

During lunch I got her to meet me behind the school by saying there was something secret going on that I needed to ask her about. She's a sucker for secrets.

"What's the matter, Ed?" she asked. She had carefully arranged herself on a bench behind the school so that none of her clothes would get dirty.

It was one thing to talk about love to guys. With Lucy it was harder. "It's about Saltz," I tried.

"Yes?"

"The thing is," I said, "he . . . Saltz, sort of . . . likes . . . someone."

Lucy, in that soft voice of hers, said, "What do you mean, Ed, when you say *like*?"

"Well, you know," I said, squirming, "*likes* . . ."

"No, I don't know."

"Loves," I got out.

She closed her eyes. "Is it me?" she said.

"No."

She acted surprised. "Who?"

"Stackpoole."

"Anabell?" That time there was puzzlement in her voice.

I nodded. "You have any idea how she feels about him?"

Lucy said, "Mary did say that Susan told her she heard Priscilla tell Jessie that, but I didn't believe it."

"How come?"

"Didn't think she was interested in that kind of thing."

"Guess she doesn't talk about it much."

"Not to me."

"To anyone?"

"Maybe to Priscilla. They're friends. Anabell's very quiet."

"I don't think the two of them know what to do about this love stuff."

She looked at me thoughtfully. "Do you?"

I shrugged.

"Maybe," she said, "we should help them."

"Right. Just because they're in love doesn't mean they can't be friends. Except . . ."

"Except what?"

"How do we do that?"

"I don't know," she admitted.

5

♡♡

NEXT DAY, during language arts class, I came up with a way to get Saltz and Stackpoole together.

It happened this way.

Romeo and Juliet is required reading for eighth grade. The play is about two teenagers, Romeo Montague and Juliet Capulet. They fall in love and want to get together. Thing is, their two families hate each other and won't let them get married. They do anyway. So a lot of people die, including them.

Anyway, a couple of days after talking to Lucy, Mrs. Bacon—our language arts teacher—was telling us that, as far as she was concerned, *Romeo and Juliet* was the greatest love story ever written with words.

"If you could just *see* the play on a stage," she said, "you would understand so much better. On stage it's real!"

Bang! I made the connection. In our class we had Saltz and Stackpoole in love, but they didn't know *how* to get together, while we, their friends (kind of a family), wanted them to. It was sort of opposite from the play, but then, we live in modern times.

This was my idea: Why not put the play on? Get Saltz to be Romeo, Stackpoole to be Juliet. If they did, they would *have* to look at each other, talk love to each other, and . . . in the play there are even a couple of kissing scenes.

What's a best friend for?

Of course, putting on a play is a big thing. We did them a lot at our school, but there was no way I could handle it myself. I needed help.

I called a meeting: Hays, Radosh, Lucy, and Priscilla Black. I asked Priscilla because she was Stackpoole's friend.

Then, just when I was about to get the meeting started, who should appear but Hamilton.

"This a secret meeting?" he demanded as he swaggered up.

"Not with you here it isn't," said Radosh.

"Yeah," I agreed. "Beat it."

"No one invited you," Priscilla chimed in.

Hamilton crossed his arms over his chest and wiggled the match stick he was chewing. "This is public property," he informed us.

I made a quick decision. The play idea wouldn't work if Hamilton went against it. He was unpredictable. He might kill the thing.

"You can stay," I told him. "Just listen."

"As long as you don't say anything dumb," he said, taking a place. He pulled out a book of matches and started to fool with them.

"This is about Saltz," I began.

"He's a slob," Hamilton put in, striking a match and throwing it into the air. "The Mount Everest of slobs."

"Come on, listen," said Priscilla. "And you're not supposed to have those."

"And Stackpoole," I tried to continue.

"What about her?" said Hamilton.

"Saltz . . . sort of . . . likes Stackpoole."

"Saltz and Stackpoole?" said Hamilton, actually putting his matches away. "You got to be kidding!" He made a big thing of rolling around, laughing and clutching his guts.

"Look," I said, getting mad, "you said you'd listen."

"Yes," said Lucy. "This is serious."

Hamilton, snorting and fussing like the jerk he always is, sat up.

"They don't know what to do about it," I went on. "They won't talk, or even look at each other." I wasn't going to mention Saltz's poems.

"What's this have to do with anything, except that they're dopes?" said Hamilton.

"In language arts," I said, trying to push on, "we're

17

reading *Romeo and Juliet*, right? My idea is, what if we actually *do* the play?"

"On the stage?" said Radosh.

"With costumes?" said Priscilla.

"Exactly. Get Saltz to play Romeo. Get Stackpoole to play Juliet. Then, they'd *have* to look at each other, right? And talk. They wouldn't even have to use their own words. And there's some . . . kissing scenes. The point is, it would really help them. What do you think?"

"Makes me want to laugh," said Hamilton.

It would have improved Hamilton's face if I'd sat on it.

"I think it's wonderful," Lucy said.

"Lot of work," offered Hays.

"How would we do it?" asked Priscilla.

"An after-school drama club," I said. "Kids have done that. I'm sure the school would let us. And they keep costumes and stuff. I'll go to Sullivan and ask permission."

"The only thing is," said Priscilla, "we'll need lots more people then just us."

"When they know what's happening," said Hays, "they'll be willing."

"You going to tell Saltz and Stackpoole?" asked Radosh.

"Right," said Priscilla. "If they guess what we're trying to do, I don't think they'll go along. Too shy."

That stumped us for a while.

"I know!" said Radosh. "Whenever we did a play before, we voted people into the parts, right?"

We nodded.

"So all we have to do," he continued, "is get Saltz and Stackpoole to come to a meeting. Then we vote them in. They won't be able to back out."

"Wouldn't catch me dead playing Romeo," Hamilton announced. "All that kissing."

"No one wants to kiss you," Priscilla informed him.

"Stuff you," returned Hamilton. He got out his matches and started to play with them again.

"I think Radosh has the answer," I said, pulling the conversation back to S and S.

"It is a lovely idea," Lucy chimed in.

In fact, they all nodded their approval except Hamilton.

"I'm against it," he told us, "unless I'm in it."

At the moment no one cared.

"You'll get a part," someone told him.

With that done we set about making plans. It was normal class politics: when and what to tell who, how not to say what to which.

6

MR. SULLIVAN, S.O.R.'s principal, is an okay guy. A bit thin maybe, pinched up and always smiling, but he'll listen if you make an appointment. The next day Lucy and I did.

"Ed, Lucy," he began. "What can I do for you?"

"In language arts," I said, "we've been reading *Romeo and Juliet*."

"William Shakespeare. The most important writer in the world," he said. "You enjoying it?"

"A lot," said Lucy. "We like it so much we want to put the play on."

He seemed astonished. "A performance?"

We nodded.

"With costumes and sets?"

"Kind of an extra project after school," I explained. "Not the whole class. Just some of us. And we'd like to use the assembly hall. Then anyone who wants to can come see it."

"Ed, *Romeo and Juliet* takes at least two and a half hours to perform."

"We'll do a short version."

"Who's going to work up the script?"

"We will," I said.

He was silent for a moment. "Are you going to direct it yourselves?"

"Sure."

"When is all this supposed to happen?" he asked.

"Couple of weeks," I said, wanting to get things going fast.

"*Two weeks?*" he said, looking startled.

"Shakespeare's pretty big in class right now," I said. "You never know what it's going to be next."

Lucy nodded.

Mr. Sullivan briefly closed his eyes. "Can you do a whole production quickly? Sets? Costumes?"

"The school stores all that," said Lucy. "We'd like to use them."

Now he nodded. "What about people to play the parts?"

"Lots."

Mr. Sullivan sat back in his chair and looked at us. "We certainly don't do enough quality things," he said. Then he reached for a big desk calendar and studied it. "In two weeks?"

Lucy and I glanced at each other, then said yes.

"It is ambitious," he said, "but . . ." He sat back full of smiles. "You're welcome to try."

We called another meeting. The only ones available were Hamilton, Radosh, and Priscilla.

"Mr. Sullivan said yes," Lucy announced. "And we can do it right away."

"What part do I get?" Hamilton demanded.

"This is for Saltz," I reminded him.

"And Stackpoole," put in Priscilla.

"It just better not be only love muck," said Hamilton. "Fighting. That's the part I want."

"You'll get it," I said. I turned to Priscilla. "Help me with the script?"

She agreed.

"Saltz for Romeo," said Hamilton. "Stackpoole for Juliet. What a bomb."

"Hamilton, no bombs."

"Just kidding."

7

UNFORTUNATELY, Mr. Sullivan told Mrs. Bacon what was going on. Next class she asked Lucy and me to stay after our bell rang.

Mrs. Bacon always wears flowery dresses, which are either military camouflage or pictures of large swamps. I never can tell which. But actually she's a nice person. I like her. She really loves what she teaches and is always enthusiastic.

She said, "I think it's wonderful that you're going to do *Romeo and Juliet*. How can I be helpful?"

Lucy and I looked at each other nervously. Mrs. Bacon, without meaning to, had a way of taking over.

"Well, actually," I tried, "we didn't want to bother you."

"Right," Lucy agreed. "It's a whole lot of work. And it was our idea."

"That's very considerate of you. But perhaps, just to get you going, it would be a good idea to let me help with the script. Such a *wonderful* play." She pressed a hand to one of the larger swamp flowers on her dress. "And it's so important to preserve the *integrity* of the immortal Bard."

"Who?"

"That's the name by which Shakespeare is known."

Neither of us knew what to say.

"Really," she continued, "I'd be delighted to do it. It's important to do Shakespeare properly."

"Mrs. Bacon," I said, trying to think fast, "remember how you said that the play was really about kids? You know, Juliet thirteen, Romeo a little older?"

"That's true. Shakespeare isn't just for all times of the day but for all ages."

"That's the whole point," I agreed. "We thought, since it's about kids, and we're doing it for kids, it's only fair that kids get to do it themselves."

"Right," Lucy chimed in, "nobody knows us more than us."

"Except him," I quickly said.

"Who is him?" said Mrs. Bacon, a bit confused.

"The Bard," I said, edging Lucy toward the door.

"And we promise," I said, as Lucy and I backed out of the room, "we'll be very dignified."

That same day, feeling we had to work fast before grown-ups butted in, Priscilla and I spent the afternoon on the script. It wasn't hard. We knew what scenes we wanted Saltz and Stackpoole to do. And during class Mrs. Bacon had gone through the play with us, making us underline famous quotes.

By the end of the day we had our version.

8

IT WASN'T long before everyone in class—everyone except Saltz and Stackpoole—knew what was happening. There were exchanges of looks, passed notes, and giggles. People kept glancing at Saltz and/or Stackpoole. Just the notion that they were in love— our first big romance—was thrilling.

Lots of people were offering to play parts or help with the production.

The only tricky part, and we all saw it, was finding a scheme to get Saltz and Stackpoole to that first meeting when parts would be chosen, then nabbing them for Romeo and Juliet.

Soon as I could, I made sure to walk home with Saltz.

The talk wasn't going anywhere in particular when I said, "If I asked you to do me a favor, would you do it?"

He said, "Depends on what it is."

I made it harder. "Don't you trust me?"

"Most times."

"Which time is this?"

He considered me. "You must want something."

"Right. I want you to say yes, no matter what, you'll do it."

He looked at me suspiciously.

"Best friends," I reminded him, trying to put on a sweet and innocent-looking face.

"Okay," he finally said, "I'll trust you."

"No matter what?"

"I said yes, didn't I? What is it?"

"I want you to be in a play."

"What's that supposed to mean?"

"We're going to put on a play, all on our own, at school. Kind of an eighth grade drama club."

"What kind of play?"

"*Romeo and Juliet.*"

That stopped him. "You're kidding."

"Honest."

"The whole thing?"

"The important parts."

He shrugged.

"Mr. Sullivan," I lied, "said if we want to do it has to be done in two weeks."

He shuffled on. "I thought you were going to ask me something hard."

"That's it." I had to keep from grinning.

27

"Want me to do the spotlight?"

"I'm not sure yet. Whatever I need. You said you would."

"No big deal."

"Remember—you promised."

He shrugged. "Fine."

I called Priscilla that night and told her how I had hooked Saltz. She told me she got Stackpoole pretty much the same way.

Simple.

We thought.

9

THE FIRST HINT that it wasn't going to be simple came when one of the guys in class, Jim Sondstrom, said to me, "Hey, Sitrow, who gets to play Romeo? Saltz or Hamilton?"

"Mind saying that again?" I asked.

"I know Saltz is your buddy," he said, "but he's no Romeo."

"It's all set up," I told him.

"You're going to have a club, right? Clubs are open to anyone, and you can't just pick who you want."

That sounded like Hamilton talking, which figured because Sondstrom was one of Hamilton's pals.

Soon as I had the chance, I faced Hamilton off in a corner. He was twisting foil around wooden matches to make little rockets. "What's this about your wanting the Romeo part?" I demanded, keeping my voice low.

29

"What about it?" he returned, not even looking at me.

"This was supposed to be for Saltz and Stackpoole."

"I thought it over," said Hamilton. "Romeo's part is neat. Lots of sword fights."

"But Saltz . . ."

"He stinks. A disgrace. We need someone good like me. And if I don't get the part, I'll tell him what's going on."

If I've thought of punching Hamilton in the mouth once, I've had the thought a million times. Not that I ever do. Two reasons: he's bigger and stronger. I turned around and went off.

After math I called a quick meeting of the committee: Hays, Radosh, Lucy, and Priscilla. I told them that Hamilton was trying to get the Romeo part.

Priscilla gave a shrug. "It's hard for people to think of Saltz as Romeo."

"Right," Radosh agreed. "For instance, he should try wearing a belt instead of hitching up his pants all the time."

"He'll clean up his act once he gets the part," I offered. "I'm sure he will."

"Why don't you try telling Saltz what's happening," Hays suggested. "Get him to campaign for the part. Then Hamilton can't blackmail you."

I shook my head. "If he knew, he wouldn't be in it at all. I know it."

"We're going to have to move fast," Radosh warned. "The longer we wait, the harder it's going to be to get Saltz and Stackpoole where we want them."

Priscilla jumped in. "Let's tell people who want to work on the play that we'll meet *this* afternoon, back of the school, right after last class."

We all agreed.

Lucy and I hurriedly went over how we'd set things up. Then, during lunch, I told Saltz that we had an organizational meeting for the drama club.

"Remember," I told him, "you promised to help."

"Sure."

"Just be there!"

"No problem."

10

♡ ♡

By 3:20 that afternoon there were twelve people out back behind the school. The exchanged looks, nudges, and pokes made it seem like we were in a warm-up session for a karate class.

I checked to see if the two most important people were there. Stackpoole was in the back row plugged into a book called *Apricots in the Attic*.

Obviously, she had no idea what was going on. When I glanced that way, Priscilla, who was sitting next to her, gave me a thumbs-up sign.

But when I looked for Saltz, I near died. He *wasn't* there. The last time I'd seen him was during lunch hour, when I told him about the meeting. I had no idea where he was.

Of course, Hamilton appeared. In spades. Somehow he had put together a costume. He wore a snap brim hat, the kind men used to wear in movies during the forties and fifties, with a long feather stuck into its band. It curled up and over his head, coming to the end of his nose like a big question mark. He also had cowboy boots into which his trouser bottoms were tucked. There was a cape, too, that looked to me like a Superman bit. But Hamilton wouldn't have chosen anyone else.

On his chest, instead of a big *S*, he had a big *R*, cut from paper and attached with pins. Romeo-man, I guess. He also had a stick for a sword.

When he walked up, people laughed and cheered. I had the sinking feeling that my candidate had just lost a few votes. And it wasn't even supposed to be a real election.

I finally called the meeting to order.

"Now, if you really want to do *Romeo and Juliet* —and I guess you're saying you do or you wouldn't be here—it has to be performed in two weeks. That's all the time we have."

I paused to look around. General agreement, but still no Saltz.

I held up a sheaf of papers. "Here's the version of the play Priscilla and I put together. It's not the whole thing. Just the important lines. No one has to learn much."

People seemed to understand.

"First thing we have to do," I continued, "is agree who is going to do the characters.

"We'll start with Juliet," I said, trying to stall.

A couple of people couldn't resist. They looked around at Stackpoole to see her reaction. She was still reading her book and sucking her hair.

"Okay," I continued. "How about some nominations for Juliet?"

Lucy, right on cue, raised her hand.

"Yes, Lucy."

"For Juliet," she said, "I nominate Anabell Stackpoole."

There it was. Everyone spun about and stared at Stackpoole to see how she'd take it. The nomination took her completely by surprise, you could tell. She actually put down her book. The hair dropped out of her mouth. And when she saw everybody looking at her, a pink glow came to her cheeks, which made her freckles look like a map of the stars.

"Anabell," I said, "do you accept the nomination?"

Stackpoole didn't glance around. She didn't smile. She didn't frown. All she did was pop out that tiny voice of hers and say, "Yes."

"Do we have a second for the nomination?"

"Second!" called Jessie Bolin.

"Any other nominations?"

Silence—all according to plan. As Stackpoole realized what had happened, her pink glow turned flaming red.

"All in favor?" I said, calling the vote.

"Aye," people called out.

"Congratulations, Anabell," I said. "You're our Juliet. Good luck."

She took the news in silence.

That was the opener. But Saltz had still not arrived.

11

♡ ♡

"OFF TO a good start," I said, trying to sound enthusiastic. Actually, I was getting very nervous.

"Any nominations for Romeo?"

Hamilton sprang to his feet. "I nominate myself," he announced.

I felt trapped by my own setup. "Seconds for Albert Hamilton?" I had to ask.

If he could have, Hamilton would have done that too. As it was, one of his buddies, Peter Marks, did it for him.

"Second!" he shouted.

"Any other nominations?"

Hays called out, "I nominate Pete Saltz."

"Where is he?" Hamilton demanded.

No one gave an answer.

"Saltz accepts," I said.

"Has to be here in person," Hamilton blustered. As soon as he said it, I knew that whatever happened to Saltz, Hamilton was behind it. Fortunately, no one listened to him.

"Second for Saltz?"

Lucy said, "I second the nomination for Peter Saltz."

"Come on," Hamilton jeered, "Saltz can't do it. It'd be a joke. All you have to do is look at him. If he's a Romeo, then I'm the man in the moon."

"Majority wins," I said. "All in favor of Hamilton for Romeo, raise your hands."

Up went the hands. I counted, then announced, "Six."

A bad feeling began to grow inside of me. There were twelve kids there. If Saltz didn't show up, it would be a tie vote. I didn't like that.

But I had to go on. "All in favor of Saltz for Romeo, raise your hands."

The people in favor of Saltz voted. I took a peek at Stackpoole and was relieved to see she was for Saltz.

"Tie vote," I said.

"He's not here," Hamilton called out. "That means it has to be me!"

It was then that Saltz, running like crazy, made his appearance, a half-eaten muffin in one hand, a bulging bag of books in the other. As he ran, he tripped over an untied shoelace. Down went his books. Down went his muffin. Red-faced and breathless, he went to gather them. "Someone jammed my locker," he said by way of explanation. "I couldn't get to my stuff."

"That's all right," I said. "You're just in time to be our last voter."

Saltz, hitching up his trousers, looked around.

"Who do you want to play the boy's lead in *Romeo and Juliet*? You or Albert Hamilton?"

"What?" said Saltz, still flustered by his late arrival.

"You going to vote for yourself or Albert Hamilton?"

No problem. Without any thought, Saltz's anti-Hamilton feelings took over. "Me," he said.

"Congratulations," I told him, "you've won the part."

"What part?"

"The part of Romeo."

Half of the people, led by Hamilton, booed. The other half, led by me, cheered. As for Saltz, I don't think he knew what was going on.

12

AFTER Romeo and Juliet, the most important character for the plot is Tybalt, Romeo's big enemy. Naturally, Hamilton wanted, and got, that part. No way I could keep him from it.

What's more, he made it clear that he wasn't going to just fool around. He *was* Saltz's (and my) enemy. Soon as he was chosen, he stood up and said, "Just want you turkeys to know, in *my* version of the play, Tybalt wins!" And he stalked off with some of his pals.

I didn't care. The main thing was done, Saltz and Stackpoole were going to do the big parts.

Saltz and I walked home together. I wasn't going to say anything about what had happened, wanting to leave it to him.

At first he kept his mouth shut. Then after a while, he said, "My being Romeo, that your idea all along?"

"Sort of . . ."

"What's that supposed to mean?"

"I was trying to be helpful."

"With what?"

"Didn't want Hamilton to get it, did you?"

"No."

"Well . . ."

He studied me carefully. "That your only reason?"

"What other reason is there?"

"You know. . . ."

"No, I don't."

"Yes, you do."

"You mean Stackpoole?"

"Yeah."

"No way," I lied cheerfully.

"Could have fooled me."

"Honest."

"Liar."

"Hey, you voted for yourself."

"I always vote against Hamilton."

"You're smart."

"Maybe."

"Don't worry. You'll be great."

"Think so?" He wiped his nose with the back of his hand.

"Know so."

More silent walking.

After a while he said. "Wonder what she feels."

"Who?"

"You know."

"Ask her."

"Forget it."

I stopped and faced him. "One of these days you're going to have to talk to her."

"Maybe."

We walked a little farther. Suddenly, he halted midstep.

"What's the matter?"

"That play has a kissing scene."

"Right," I said, easy as I could manage. "Two of them."

A look of real trouble came over his face. "I never kissed a girl before," he said. "Not that way."

"Right . . ."

"I mean, before, you know, like in the sixth grade, you only kissed girls you *didn't* like."

"This is eighth grade," I reminded him.

"I don't know if I can."

"Come on, you'll be fine."

"How many people do you think will come?"

"Ten, twelve, if we're lucky."

"Think they'll watch?" he said, his voice almost a whisper.

"That way no one can accuse you of being sneaky," I said.

For the rest of the way home neither of us talked. Then, after we reached his place, and he was about to go inside, he turned and said, "You *did* set me up, Sitrow. Admit it."

"Well . . ."

"Yes or no?"

"Maybe."

"I thought we were best friends."

"Aren't we?"

He looked at me, steely-eyed. "Let's see what happens."

13

♡ ♡

NEXT AFTERNOON we all got together in a small room in the basement. But no sooner did we get there than in came Mrs. Bacon.

"Here I am, ready to help," she announced. "What would you like me to do?"

We sat there not knowing what to say. She didn't seem to notice.

Finally, I got up. "Could I speak to you privately, Mrs. Bacon?"

"Of course!"

We stepped out into the hall. "Mrs. Bacon, I think I better tell you what this is really about."

She frowned.

"You know how grown-ups are always saying kids these days can't do anything for themselves. That all we do is watch television sitcoms and only think about sex and stuff like that."

"A lot of people do say such things," Mrs. Bacon admitted.

"Well, there's nothing more important than Shake-speare, right?"

"Yes. . . ."

"See, if we do this ourselves we can show people how mature we are. We appreciate your help. Really. We just want to do it alone."

"I hadn't thought of it that way," she said with an understanding smile. "And you're right. It will set a wonderful example for the rest of the school. And the community. But remember, if you do need help, just ask."

Off she went.

I went back into the room. Everybody looked at me. "It's cool," I announced. "I told her we could handle everything ourselves."

Except right away we discovered we had forgotten to choose a director.

No one volunteered, not even Hamilton. Getting impatient, he was having sword fights with his own shadow.

It was Priscilla who suggested Lucy. "You don't have a part," she said, "and anyway, someone has to be in charge."

"I don't know what to do," Lucy pleaded.

Once more I got up. "Let me talk to you a minute."

Now Lucy and I went out into the hall.

"Look," I said, "you know more about people being in love than any of us, right? I mean you act old and all. And that's what this is all about, right? You could tell them how to act. Know what I'm saying?"

She said nothing, just looked at me.

"I mean, you're the most experienced."

"Do you think so?"

"Aren't you?"

After a moment she said she'd do the job. I gave her the script.

She looked at it. "Ed . . ."

"What?"

"Don't you think we need more than one copy?"

The rest of that afternoon was taken up with trying to get the copier in the school library to work. And finding nickels to put into the machine when it did work.

Show business is very exciting.

14

♡ ♡

ONCE MORE we gathered in the small basement room, sitting on little chairs, scripts on our laps.

Lucy said we might as well start by reading the play through. In fact, for the next two rehearsals people only read their parts out loud. Except every time someone read a line, or *tried* to read a line, Lucy had to say, "I can't hear you."

Stackpoole shrank down under any criticism, even soft criticism like Lucy's.

Saltz would just say something like "Humph" and not change a thing he was doing, except maybe get red in the face.

The only one who could boom it out was, of course, Hamilton. He acted as if he was the most important character. If he'd had the chance, I think he would have called the play "Albert and Juliet."

Then we finally got to the first of the scenes between Romeo and Juliet. It's when they first see each other. The point of the whole production. Everybody got very quiet.

Stackpoole and Saltz read their lines as if they were checking the phone book for spelling mistakes. They wouldn't even *look* at each other. To watch them was like rooting for two teams who never got on the field.

The next day was the same. I began to wonder if the whole thing wasn't a mistake.

Lucy had the same thought. She asked me to stay after rehearsal.

"Ed," she began, "how do you think it's going?"

"Not so great," I admitted.

"They're not showing very much feeling for the lines, are they? They don't seem to understand much about being in love. I don't think they've looked at each other once in two days."

"I know."

"I don't understand it," said Lucy, who was really upset. "Whenever you see people in love on TV they act so happy, or, you know, they get to hate each other. You have a choice. These two don't do *anything.*"

"I guess it takes more time," I said.

"We don't have much time," she reminded me.

"Maybe when we get on stage it will be better," I offered.

"How are the sets and costumes coming along?" she asked.

"Perfect," I assured her. "Nothing to worry about. Everything will be ready on schedule."

The truth was, I hadn't started on them.

15

♡ ♡

I REMEMBERED something that I hoped would give us a break. The month before, the seventh grade had presented a play they'd written themselves. It was about olden times, which is when *Romeo and Juliet* takes place.

Since we needed scenery for our play, and they no longer needed theirs, I got the idea that with a little paint we could save lots of work by using what they had made.

I went to see Mr. Rhodes, the teacher in charge of that production. I told him we had set up an eighth grade drama club and wondered if we could use his old set.

"Sure," he said, "help yourself. It's still stacked up in the basement."

I thanked him and started off.

"Ed!" he called. I turned back.

"Where are you going to do your play?"

"In the assembly hall."

"You going to be running things?"

"Sure."

"Just make sure you practice with the electrical switches. It can get confusing. And watch out for the curtain. It's erratic."

I promised I'd be careful.

I went to check the sets. They looked fine to me. Then I tracked down Sam Pettry.

Sam is a very relaxed kind of person. No matter how crazy things go, nothing seems to trouble him. Since there was a whole lot to do, and I was beginning to feel pressure about getting things done, I asked him if he'd help with the sets and stuff.

"No problem," he said.

I told him about the sets that Mr. Rhodes said we could use as well as what we needed. "You read the play, right? So you know where it takes place."

"No problem," he said again.

"Okay," I said, liking his approach to things. "Do whatever you can."

"No problem."

Like I said, laid back.

Costumes were another matter. For that job I went to Jessie Bolin. A lot of people think Jessie is a little weird. I don't. True, she sometimes wears so much jewelry (necklaces, bracelets, and pins) she looks and rattles like a Christmas tree gone wild. And yes, it's also true that the colors she wears—purple, orange, and green—are bright. But she is *by far* the most interesting-looking person in class. And she wants to be a fashion designer. When she offered to help with the play, I said yes right away.

Our school is always doing plays, so we have a large closet of costume stuff. Jessie and I went to check it out.

I recognized costumes from *The Wizard of Oz, Peter Pan,* and *The Vampire of Central High.* Jessie found things from *Columbus Discovers America* and *The Search for Planet X,* as well as *The Adventures of Santa Claus.*

I could tell Jessie liked what she saw. She kept saying things like "Wow! Far out! Too much! Great!" When I left her, she was sitting on the floor of the closet staring up at a moth-eaten King Kong outfit.

Like Pettry would have said: "No problem."

16

♡ ♡

I GOT some people for props and makeup and to work on the sets during the actual performance. That left me free to do the one thing I had to do myself, the stage.

Our assembly hall had once been a gym. You can still smell it. But then the school built a whole new wing for sports and, in the old gym, a sort of a stage.

Most of the time gray folding chairs are set up there. They get removed only for dances or things like science fairs. It's the sixth grade's job to put them up or down, which they like because you get to make a lot of noise.

As for the stage, it's a raised platform, three feet off the floor, at the far end of the room, the whole width.

A fringe of curtains hangs from the top, hiding rows of white, blue, and red stage lights.

At each side of the stage are more curtains. They

don't move but make places that are called wings. People can wait there without being seen before going out on the stage.

It was from there that I was supposed to run the whole show. You can see the stage clearly from there, as well as the audience through a peephole.

The regular curtain, which goes up and down, not back and forth, is on a big, heavy roller. The lifting and dropping is done by an electric motor. Push the labeled switch up, and up it goes. Down, down.

I gave it a try. The sucker dropped like a bag of bricks.

I flipped the switch up. The curtain started up fast, slowed, then stopped halfway. Next second it came crashing down. I gave the switch another try. That time it worked perfectly. Mr. Rhodes was right. I would need practice.

Next to the curtain switch are light switches, maybe nine or ten of them. Each switch has a label stuck on so you can tell what ones you are turning on and off.

I started with one labeled Stage Lights Blue. Right away, the blue lights over the stage came on. By twisting the switch I could get it to go from dim to bright. I tried Stage Lights Red and got red. And I did the white ones too. No problem.

There are switches for the auditorium lights as well, and one to lower the movie screen. And then there's a spotlight switch.

That spotlight is in the hall, mounted high up on a platform. To get to it you have to climb a ladder built into the wall.

The spotlight switch works differently from the other lights. When you turn it, a small signal light comes on by the spotlight. That tells the person working there that he can turn on the spot and aim the light where it needs to go.

The point is I had to get another person to run it. Trouble was, I had run out of volunteers.

That night I made calls but couldn't get anyone. There were actually people out there who were interested in doing things other than *Romeo and Juliet*.

That's when I turned to Hays's sister. Her name is Betsy. She was in the sixth grade, and she had a crush on me. I don't know why. Kind of embarrassing. Whenever I went over to Hays's place, she would hang around.

Anyway, after giving up trying to get someone from my class to help with the spotlight I felt a little desperate. Being desperate is when you think a friend's kid sister who has a crush on you might be helpful.

I called Hays and told him what the problem was. I asked him if he minded my asking his sister for help. "Are you kidding?" he said. "She'd love it."

"Okay," I said, "better let me speak to her."

"Sure."

There was a long wait. After that came running steps and an awful crash. Then I heard a frantic, muffled "Where are my glasses?"

("Right in front of you, dummy.")

("Where! I can't see them!")

("Here. In your hand.")

("They're broken!")

("You don't have to see him. He just wants to talk to you.")

There was some more waiting. "Hello?" I tried.

("Say something!" came Hays's voice again. "He's on the phone!")

"Betsy?"

"Yes." It was one word, but it was a bit breathless.

"This is Ed."

"Oh, hi."

"You okay?"

("Will you speak to the guy!")

"Fine."

("Your glasses are on upside down!")

"Did your brother tell you about the play we're putting on?"

("Would you go away so I can talk to him!") "I think so."

"We need someone to run the spotlight in the assembly hall. You know, from the back. Could you do it?"

("Go away!")

("It's a free country. I can stand here.")

"Me?"

"I'd really appreciate it. I can't get anyone else."

("Would you go *away!*")

"I could try."

"That would be great."

("Tell him you have a crush on him.")

("Leave me alone!")

"Betsy?"

"You'd have to teach me how."

("Teach you what?")

"Cinch," I assured her.

"Okay." ("Would you stop trying to . . .")

The phone went dead.

I wasn't sure, but I think she had said yes.

17

NEXT MORNING, when Saltz and I walked to school, I noticed that things were a little different with him. He didn't look different or act different. He shuffled along as usual, now and again stopping to hitch his pants, tie a shoelace, fix a sock, all the stuff that had broken down since leaving his house fifteen minutes before.

No, the difference was he was talking to himself.

"What did you say?" I finally asked.

"Lines," he informed me. "Lines from the play I'm supposed to learn." And again he said, "I swear a blue beauty this night."

After a moment I figured it out. "Try, 'I ne'er saw true beauty till this night.' "

"I was close," he said and tried it again. That time he was nearer.

We continued walking, and he went on mumbling lines to himself. I kept having the feeling that some of them were a little mixed up, but I wasn't going to say. I had something else on my mind.

Finally, I got up my nerve. I said, "Don't you think it's about time you talked to her?"

He considered. "Directly?"

"Right. To her face."

He shook his head.

"You're going on stage today," I reminded him.

"I know."

"How about noticing her—or at least pretending that you notice her—a little?"

"Maybe . . ."

"Look," I said, "I know I've never done any of this love stuff before. But it seems to me that if you're going to love someone, well, one of these days—it must be a rule—you have to at least look at her."

He shook his head. "You don't know what it's like."

"Okay. I don't. You tell me."

He grew thoughtful. "Hard to say," he said.

"Give it a shot. . . ."

He stopped and looked off into the distance. Then, without facing me, he tapped his chest a few times. "It's . . . it's as if . . . inside . . . there was a . . . whole . . . peanut butter cookie . . . inside. You haven't eaten it. But it's *there*. All the time. Tasting good. And it . . . doesn't go away. It just . . . stays

. . . all the time." Once more he tapped his chest, then turned to me. "Get it?"

"Fine," I told him. "Pretend she's a cookie, but look at her."

As we approached the last corner before school, I saw Hamilton. From the way he was watching I was sure he had been waiting for us to arrive. I gave Saltz a nudge. He looked up.

"He doesn't bother me," Saltz said, and we kept on. But as we went by Hamilton called out, " 'Tis he, that villain Romeo!"

We couldn't let that pass.

"What's bugging you?" I challenged.

"Just wanted to let your Romeo friend know he can still back out. He's going to look like a bucket of gross."

"Can't take second place, can you?" I threw back. Saltz, who was eyeing Hamilton, kept quiet.

"I'm just saying," Hamilton went on, "if you go on with it, you're going to be the laughing stock of school. A disaster."

"Forget it," I said and tried to lead Saltz off before a real fight started. Saltz has a temper.

Instead, Saltz swung around and began to shout lines from the play at Hamilton. "I do protest," he said, "I never injured thee!"

That made Hamilton blink. Me too.

Saltz went on. "All the same, I bite my thumb at

58

you!" And he did. Hamilton, for once, was speech-
less.

I never thought Shakespeare could be useful like
that. I was impressed.

18

♡ ♡

LUCY'S JOB was to tell the actors where and how to move around. She called this blocking. I'm not sure why it's called that, except maybe it was because the actors acted like blockheads.

She kept trying to get them to do things right. "Peter, when you say that, I think you should walk toward the edge of the stage. No, the other way."

Or "Peter, don't turn your back to the audience or you'll fall off the stage!"

Or "Albert, try that again. You don't have to run. And I wish you'd put away those matches."

That's the way it went for everybody. Boredom times six. But finally, the big moment came, the first time Saltz and Stackpoole *had* to face each other and speak their lines. It's at this big Saturday night dance where they meet.

The people watching grew hushed. Drama filled the air.

"Peter," said Lucy, speaking from a seat in the hall, "this is where you see Juliet for the first time. It's, you know, love at first sight. The inside max."

"Now?" asked Saltz, peering out from behind the curtain wings where he had been hiding.

"Yes, now."

Saltz got out on stage, clumped around, and finally said a few lines. I was sitting in the first row but didn't hear a word.

"Peter," Lucy tried, "you can't fall in love at first sight unless you *see* her. Try turning around and facing Juliet. Where is Anabell?"

Stackpoole was hiding behind the other wing. She emerged, slowly.

"Anabell," Lucy continued. "I think you should take the hair out of your mouth. Look at Peter."

There they were. Facing each other at last.

"Saltz!" cried Hays, "open your eyes!"

And from somewhere Hamilton bellowed, "And put your chewing gum behind your ear!"

Lucy decided to cut the rehearsal short. She wouldn't talk to me. In fact nobody would talk to me except Betsy, Hays's sister.

"Ed," she said after everybody else was gone.

I hadn't even known she was at the rehearsal. She had been in the back of the hall all along. With those glasses of hers, high-neck sweater, and jeans, she looked like a baby turtle.

"Oh, hi," I said.

"Do you still want me to do the spotlight?"

"Sure."

"Could you show me how?"

I had other things on my mind. "How about tomorrow?"

"Okay."

Ten o'clock that night Saltz called me. "I have to ask you something," he said.

"Go ahead."

"Something in the play."

"Anything you want."

"Hard to say."

"Just try."

"Look, I have to . . ."

"What?"

"You know . . ."

"Just say it!" I cried.

"Well, I . . . Romeo . . . have to . . . kiss . . . Juliet."

"Right. Twice."

There was a long pause. Then Saltz said, "I don't know how."

"How what?"

"I just told you."

"Kissing?"

"Yeah. Kissing."

"Didn't you ever kiss anyone before?"

"Not like this. You?"

"No," I admitted.

"Okay then. How am I supposed to do it?"

"You just . . . do. You must have seen it on TV a million, billion times. That's all they do."

"If you're so sure, you explain how."

"Okay, basically, you . . . scrunch up your lips. . . ."

"Go on."

"Sort of suck . . ."

"Suck?"

"Will you listen! You do those things. Both of them. Then . . . Come on. You know!"

"Honest. I don't. I got to thinking about it, and suddenly I realized I didn't. I mean, maybe they tell girls, but no one tells boys."

"Okay. Fine. You do all those things I told you, right . . ?"

"Scrunch and suck. . . ."

"Right, and then . . ."

"Go on."

"You put your mouth on . . . hers."

"What if she spits?"

"Will you listen!"

"Or burps. I mean, it's weird, isn't it?"

"Can't be."

"Why?"

"Because people—most of them—like it."

"Maybe they just *say* that. Maybe it's just a fad. There are always fads. They go away."

"Saltz, it's in the play. You have to do it."

63

"It's going to be hard."

I thought for a moment. "Does your sister have a Cabbage Patch Kid?"

"I think so."

"Practice on one of them."

"That's sick. Really sick."

"Then try your dog."

"Sometimes, Sitrow, you really are creepy!"

"I'm trying to help. I'm your friend!"

"Some friend!" he cried and hung up.

19

PEOPLE didn't know their lines. Or they forgot what they were supposed to be doing on stage, like which direction to walk. True, sometimes they forgot their lines as well which way to go.

On the plus side there was some progress in getting Stackpoole to look at Saltz. Also progress in getting Saltz to look at Stackpoole. The hard part was getting them to do it at the same time.

As for the famous kissing scenes . . . whenever we got to those parts everybody would pay close attention. Perfect silence. Saltz and Stackpoole would inch forward, sort of say their lines (mostly not), look here, there, everywhere, but not at each other. Then, just as they were supposed to get very close (a kiss!), Saltz would have to tie his shoe. Or Stackpoole would blow her nose. They never got to it. Not once! It was maddening.

If Saltz and Stackpoole underacted, Hamilton

overacted, trying to upstage Saltz by grandstanding, fooling around, telling everybody the whole thing would go up in a ball of fire—anything to make himself the center of attention. I kept telling myself it was all going to work out.

After one rehearsal I ducked out to avoid Hays's sister and went to the local library to get some books for some project I was working on.

As I went toward the kids' room, I happened to notice Stackpoole off in a corner by herself, as usual. She was sitting on a big soft chair, legs tucked underneath. One pile of books was on a table in front of her; another pile was by her side. A book was in her hand. It was called *Return to Ecstasy*.

I stopped to look. She wasn't reading. She was staring off somewhere, nibbling on her hair.

I felt like going over to her and offering some words of encouragement, but I felt awkward, not sure what to say.

I went to get the stuff I needed.

Later, when I was all involved in my own work, I realized someone was standing right next to me. I looked up. It was Stackpoole.

"Oh, hi," I said.

She was looking very serious. "Can I talk to you?" she said.

"Sure. Something the matter?"

"It's this play. . ." she said. Her voice was very small.

"It's going great, isn't it?" I offered.

"I don't think I'm very good," she said.

"You're fine."

She shook her head. "I'd like to be better," she said.

"That's why we're rehearsing," I said.

"It was your idea to do the play, wasn't it?"

I nodded yes.

"Thank you."

"Oh, well . . ."

"I just wanted to let you know that I am trying. I'd like to do it well. It means a lot to me."

Before I could say anything, she turned around and marched out of the building.

I realized I didn't really know her at all.

20

♡ ♡

As we approached the performance date, a couple of kids put on an advertising campaign. Signs began appearing all over the school.

ROMEO ♡ JULIET!
The Bard is back and
S.O.R. has got him!

ROMEO AND JULIET
Together (and alive!)
at last

Naturally, the date and time of the performance was given. We wondered how many would show up. Lucy and I decided if we got ten it would be good enough.

A couple of times I received messages from Mr. Sullivan saying he would like to come and watch a rehearsal. When he didn't come, and we were getting to the end of things, he promised to come to the dress rehearsal.

Then there were the moments when Mrs. Bacon would appear. Soon as she came in everything stopped. "How's it going?" she'd say.

"Fine," we'd always answer.

"Looks good," she'd say, not that she saw anything. "Call on me when you need help," she'd add. Tipping me a wink of understanding, she'd leave.

Every now and then Lucy would ask me how the sets and costumes were coming along. I kept telling her that everything was fine. Not that I ever did check it all out. The way I saw it, my job was to stay with Saltz.

And faithfully, after every rehearsal, Betsy would show. Each time she'd ask me if I could show her how to work the spotlight. A real nuisance. Finally, I said, "Betsy, do you see that balcony up there?" I pointed to it.

She turned to look. "*Up there?*"

"Right. That's where you have to be. Why don't you go on up and have a look. Get a feel for it."

She didn't say anything. Just stared at it. "How high is that?"

"I don't know," I admitted. "Sixteen feet, maybe."

"Is that where the light is?"

"I told you, remember?"

Again she looked from me to the balcony. "Oh," she said, and drifted off in that direction.

As for the rest of the lights, I figured that with the labels in place there was nothing to worry about. True, the curtain continued to be a problem, so I did work on that. While I hadn't quite gotten the hang of it, I knew I would.

21

MR. SULLIVAN showed up on the day before the performance, just as our dress rehearsal was about to get under way.

He sat on the edge of the stage, legs dangling in the air. "So you're going to do William Shakespeare's *Romeo and Juliet*." He smiled and nodded.

"Sorry I've not been able to watch any of your rehearsals," he continued. "But Mrs. Bacon has kept me informed. She says you're doing a fine job.

"I won't be able to stay today because I have a board meeting. But, Ed, you've certainly done a fine job putting this all together. So quickly too. I'm very impressed." He nodded, smiled. "I've invited the school board, the superintendent, and of course, your parents. I know that will please you." Smile. Nod.

"As you know," he continued, "it's been years since we've done Shakespeare at S.O.R. It's a serious undertaking. A real responsibility. What you do on this stage will have a considerable impact on your fellow students. S.O.R. is counting on you!"

He left, smiling and nodding.

Actually, the dress rehearsal wasn't really a *dress* rehearsal. Jessie Bolin, who was in charge of costumes, had pole-vaulting practice that afternoon, so she couldn't make it. She did tell me everything was, and I quote, "fantastic," so I didn't worry.

As for the sets, Sam Pettry had them ready and on stage. I knew I could count on him. Everybody was impressed, too.

I did ask Hays where his sister was. Ever since she realized where the spotlight was located I hadn't seen her. He promised he'd get her to show up.

Then we worked through the final rehearsal. It was pretty good. People mostly remembered their lines and what to do. They play made sense. The only problem was that Stackpoole and Saltz continued to be shy of each other.

Still, we were excited when the rehearsal was over.

After the others had left, Lucy and I remained for a moment.

"Looks great," I told her. "You did a good job."

"Ed, do you think they'll look at each other during the play?"

"I promise," I said. I believed it, too.

22

Romeo and Juliet, our version anyway, was supposed to get under way at 3:15 in the afternoon.

A couple of times during the day I tried to get into the hall but couldn't. The doors were locked. Since I had to get to classes I didn't have the time to track down the custodian.

All day I kept hearing from kids about the production. Some wanted to know about the Saltz–Stackpoole part. A few even promised to show up. That was a relief. I had been worried that the only ones we'd get were the people Mr. Sullivan had invited.

About fifteen minutes before three o'clock—in my last class—I decided I couldn't hold back any more. I told the teacher I had to get to the bathroom. When he gave me permission to leave, I took off.

I went straight to the assembly hall, only to find the doors still locked.

That time I did search for the custodian. By the

time I got him to come to the hall the doors were already open. What's more, Hamilton was there.

It being five to three (twenty minutes before curtain time), I had to rush back to homeroom and check out with Mrs. Misakian, only to slam back.

No sooner did I get into the hall than everybody else came, too. All the people connected with the play busting in like popcorn on the pop. Yelling. Shouting. Lost things. Found things. Broken things. Cries for help. "Where's my wig?" "Where's my sword?" "What happened to my eyebrows?" And since I was in charge of the actual performance, everybody kept coming to me for help. I hardly had a moment to myself.

I did manage to check the stage set. Things looked fine.

It wasn't until close to ten after three that I was able to check out the electrical switches. I wanted to run through them a final time. In particular, I needed to practice with the curtain.

I started to put my hand to the switch labeled Red Stage Lights, only to draw back. Something wasn't right. Every one of the switch labels—the labels that showed which switch switched which light—had been changed. No, not changed. The labels were *gone*.

I couldn't believe what I was not seeing.

Trying to remember what was what, I flicked on a switch, hoping for the red stage lights. Nothing on

74

stage changed. But there was a near riot backstage where people were putting on costumes and makeup. "Lights! Lights! Get the lights!" came the screams.

I threw back the switch I had switched, then tried another, hoping for the spotlight. At least I thought it was the spotlight.

It was the curtain, and it moved like a rocket heading for Mars.

Feeling something close to panic, I stood there trying to think what to do. Out of the corner of my eye I saw Hamilton sneaking a look at me, a grin strung ear to ear. I took a step in his direction, screaming, "Hamilton!" but he ran off.

It was five minutes before we were supposed to begin.

"Ed!" I heard. Mrs. Misakian's voice. I rushed onto the stage. She was standing out front.

"Mrs. Misakian," I began, "Hamilton switched the . . ."

"Ed," she said, cutting me off, "I've just been given a note from the front office. Amy Jefferson got ill during gym and had to go right home. I think she was supposed to be in your play."

"You're kidding!"

"You'll have to get someone else to do the part."

"Mrs. Misakian, the lights . . ."

"Ed, Mr. Sullivan wants me to meet the school board president in his office. He's coming to see the play. Isn't that exciting? I'll see you after the performance." She hurried away.

"Ed!"

I looked around to see who was calling me.

"I'm here!" It was Betsy, my spotlighter, calling from the rear light balcony. In the dark I could only barely make her out. "What is it?"

"I dropped my glasses."

I ran to the back of the hall and began to search, finding them by stepping on them. "Got 'em," I announced.

"Can you bring them up? I can't see without them and I'm afraid to climb down."

"They're broken."

"Completely?"

"Just the glass parts," I said, not wanting to explain my contribution.

"What do you want me to do? I can't see much."

"Point in the general direction of the stage." I turned to go.

"Ed!"

"What?"

"Which way is the stage?"

At that moment a voice cried, "Audience coming in!"

I turned to watch the assembly hall doors burst open. A tidal wave of kids came roaring in. It looked like the whole school had decided to show up.

23

♡♡

I RAN backstage, still needing to find someone to do Amy Jefferson's part. At the moment I couldn't even remember what character she played.

"Anybody got a program?" I asked. A copy was thrust into my hand.

```
      SUB LIME and TraGic HISTORY OF
             ROMEO AN JULIET
                    by
    The IMMORAL wILLIA m "Shakespeare"
   Adopted for S.O.r Middle school by
       Ed Sitrow and Priscilla Black
                 Directed by Lucy Niblet
          Stage manager by ed SitroW
                   CAST
       (The order of disappearance)
   Chorus (one person)...David Eliscue
   Romeo ................Peter Saltz
   Tybalt ...............Albert Hamilton
```

```
Mercutio ...............David Gullette
Prince of Verona......Ralph Porter
Juliet's ma ..........Amy Jeffrerson
And her father........Peter Barish
Mercutio ..............Tom Hays
Bath Asar .............Paul DuBois
Fryer Laurence .......Tom Hays
Juliet ...............Anabell Stackpoole
Nurse .................Priscilla Black
Ben Volvo ....?????...Ronald Radosh
Party People ............Peter Marks, Jim
          Sondstrom, Mary Davis
          Jessie Bolin, C. Huber
```

The play takes place mostly in Italian but also a few other places.

Thanks to M.r Rhodes and the 7 grade for letting us use the set of their play <u>GEORGE WASHINGTON CROSSING THE DELAWARE</u> BY the 7 grade

```
Stage hands= Eliscue, Root, BoliN
spot lights.................Betsy Hays
Sets ......Sam Pettry ..>>>>>>>
make up..By themselves
Props .................Elizabeth Miles
Costumes ..............Jessie Bolin
```
Program writ by MARGARET FITZSIMMONS on anapple comp

By the time I had finished working through that masterpiece, it was past our promised starting time. Worse, the audience was sounding like a rampaging gang of morning garbage collectors getting impatient.

I peeked out. The special section for visitors was full. School board, parents, and for all I knew, Shakespeare himself.

And right then Mr. Sullivan appeared backstage. "Ed," he said, "I want to make a few remarks before you begin."

He turned to go. I was so unhinged I forgot all about Amy Jefferson's replacement.

Mr. Sullivan went to the front of the hall.

"We have something very special this afternoon," he began. "A play by William Shakespeare.

"As we all know, Shakespeare is the most important writer in the English language. It is therefore particularly exciting to have one of his plays presented here today. I can't tell you how much pleasure it gives me to know that a group of your schoolmates —all on their own, simply because they enjoyed the play—decided to put on a performance. It speaks well of S.O.R.

"It also speaks well of you that you chose to see this great work of literature.

"I'm sure that if you pay strict attention, you will learn a great deal."

He took his seat to a blast of applause.

Meanwhile, in the wings, in the dark, I was trying to see the light switches, trying to decide which one to pull, trying to figure out what would happen when I did.

24

NOTHING HAPPENED. Nothing at all. And after a while, still more of nothing happened. I couldn't remember how the light switches went. "Get me a flashlight!" I cried.

But feeling I couldn't stall any more, I flicked a switch. The curtain started to rise. I flicked some more. It crashed with a thump.

The audience began to titter.

A flashlight was shoved into my shaking hand. I managed to place a little light on the switchboard and made a guess as to the spotlight switch. I clicked it and took a look out front. It worked. Sort of.

A circle of bright light—the spotlight—began to glide silently around the auditorium and the curtain. It went up, down, here, there, like a baby UFO that had lost its mother and wanted to go home. My feelings exactly.

Now the audience began to giggle. Some people

began to clap in rhythm. Sweat trickled down my back.

"Need some help?" I heard Hamilton say right behind me.

"Get out of here!" I yelled.

"Suit yourself," he said, laughing as he went.

I threw some switches. That time everything went dark. The audience moaned.

We *had* to get moving. "Eliscue!" I called. "You ready?"

"I'm just . . . ouch!" he yelled. In the dark he had slammed his knee into a post.

The audience greeted this cry of pain with laughter. More people began to applaud in a steady beat. At last I got what I thought were the stage lights, the blue ones, anyway. I didn't care. I got the curtain up. At least people could see the set.

This is what they saw: On either side of the stage were two log cabins. Not real ones, but pictures painted on canvas flats. Each cabin was crusted with snow and ice. A few naked-looking trees (on other flats) stood about. Snow and ice (Christmas tree tinsel) dangled. To my horror, the blue lights somehow cut through the painted-over sign on one of the cabin doors. It read: GEORGE WASHINGTON'S HEAD-QUARTERS.

I flipped off the blue lights and managed to turn on the red ones. The sign vanished. But under the red light all that snow and ice looked like pink frosting on a candy-land village.

"Get going!" I called to Eliscue. He went, managing, by some miracle, not to bump into anything else.

The spotlight found him, dressed like a sailor. It also blinded him. He put up a hand to shield his eyes. It made him look like he was about to discover land.

He spoke, pointing to the snow and ice:

"The day is hot, the Capulets abroad

And, if we meet, we shall not 'scape a brawl;

For now, these hot days, is the mad blood stirring."

He bowed. Applause. Off he came, intact.

The spotlight began to wander around the stage again.

"Who's next?" I demanded, turning to the actors who were standing there acting confused because of my confusion, not to mention their own.

I turned off all the lights, then put them on, during which time the movie screen came down. I got it up.

"Go for it!" came a suggestion from the audience.

Saltz went for it first. Or rather, he backed on for it, only to realize that he was actually in front of a large crowd. He turned to face them and show off his costume.

It was the first time I saw it, too.

Saltz's costume consisted, from the bottom up, of long, pointy, turned-up-toe shoes. At the end of each shoe were bells. Every time he took a step, they jingled.

He also had on a pair of bright purple and very baggy tights. These tights sagged so much at the knees it looked as if his legs, like candles, were melting. Every few steps (bells jingling) he had to hitch them up.

There was also a bright yellow jacket whose sleeves were too short. By about three inches. This jacket would have been impossible to button around Saltz's middle. Fortunately, Saltz wasn't into buttoning.

A stick sword was attached to his side.

Finally, on his head was a little pillbox of a red hat, complete with a glittering Shriner's badge. This hat had a long black tassel that kept falling in front of his face like a limp windshield wiper. When he spoke his lines, he had to keep brushing it aside.

"You're supposed to be on!" I cried to the other characters.

25

THE SCENE was supposed to be the fancy-dress ball at the Capulets' house, the home of Juliet's mom and dad. It looked more like a surprise costume party in a national forest. You couldn't tell what was going on—or where—in front of the log cabins with the ice dripping, that hot day in Italy so many years ago.

Some people wore tights. Some trousers. Some girls had dresses. Others had robes. Hamilton was in a tin-can getup that was either from last year's production of *The Search for Planet X* or the Tin Woodsman's costume from *The Wizard of Oz*.

As for Stackpoole . . . She had a white dress with a very long tail. It stretched twice the length of her height. People kept stepping on it, so that any time she moved she had to yank at it with both hands. Between keeping the hair out of her face and pulling her dress free, she was a continuous nervous jiggle.

Next to her was Priscilla, who, since she was playing the role of Nurse, had on a nurse's uniform. It was complete with a nurse's cap that had a large red cross. Around her neck was a stethoscope. She kept hovering over Stackpoole, as if Stackpoole was about to faint and fall down. Actually, I think that part was true.

Anyway, there they were, on stage at last. Except they just stood there, looking like they were hanging out at a mall. Meanwhile, the spotlight was trying to find someone.

When Saltz realized the light was on him, he began to act. That is, he hitched up his tights, tried to stand tall, even as he brushed the tassel away from his mouth. Then he gave a look in Stackpoole's direction. She was looking at the floor, her hair over her face. He placed one hand on his heart, and with the other, pointed at Stackpoole. Then he said: "What lady's . . ."

He pushed the tassel away.

"What lady's that? I never saw true beauty till this night."

That line was Hamilton's cue.

He didn't just take it, he grabbed it. Armor all a-clank, he stepped forward. From his belt he pulled a long, long stick. His sword. It was so long it took two hands to haul it out. Once he got it out, he slashed the air a few times, which caused the sword to snap. The thing dangled like a crooked finger.

People on stage started to crack up.

Ditto the audience.

Grinning for all he was worth, Hamilton pointed his broken sword at Saltz and said: "Ho! 'Tis he, that villain Romeo!"

Radosh, playing the part of Benvolio, stepped up behind Saltz. Near as I could tell, Radosh was dressed like a Chinese peasant.

Saltz turned to him. Using one hand to keep the tassel out of his mouth, the other hand to point at Stackpoole, he said: "Is she a catapult?"

Radosh, not understanding—nobody else did either—said, "What?"

Saltz must have heard what he himself had spoken. He blotched red, shook his head (and tassel) and repeated the line correctly: "Is she a Capulet?"

Having gotten the line off right, he walked off stage, toe bells jangling.

Now it was Stackpoole's turn. As Saltz left the stage, she turned to Priscilla, and said: "Nurse! What's he that now is going out the door?"

Priscilla replied: "His name is Romeo, and a Montague, the only son of your great enemy."

At that point Stackpoole was supposed to take a dramatic step forward. Unfortunately, someone was standing on her dress again. She tried to move. Couldn't. Desperately, she turned and gave a yank. With a mighty rip, the dress came free.

Still, she came downstage and put her hand where her heart was supposed to be, though, in all that costume it must have been hard to find. Then she said: "Then I must love a loaded enemy."

Hamilton's turn. He came forward, standing right in front of Stackpoole, which he wasn't supposed to do. No one could see her. All the same, he made a few more passes with his broken sword.

That was *my* cue. I reached for the curtain switch and gave it a flick. What I did was turn lights on in the auditorium. The cast stood there, looking at the crowd out front with something that seemed like terror. From the stage came a loud whisper, "Turn off the lights."

I flicked another switch. Down came the curtain. The audience cheered.

End of act one.

26

HAMILTON appeared, pleasure dripping from him like a hot ice cream cone. He put an arm around Saltz and said, "Want me to play your part, buddy? I've got it memorized."

People were watching.

Saltz looked at him, at me, at the other kids. Finally, his eyes came to rest on Stackpoole, who was peering at him from somewhere in the middle of her costume. Maybe nobody else noticed, but I sure did: they had looked at each other at last!

Saltz said, "I'm doing it."

The audience meanwhile, not knowing about the drama going on backstage, wanted to see some drama *on* stage. We began to hear calls of, "Let's go. Second act!"

"Get the sets fixed," I called to the stagehands.

It took a while. Two painted trees toppled over. One flat broke. General racket and confusion. But after a while we were in good shape again.

I got hold of some switches and gave them a flip. The curtain shot up. Some light came on, lurid purple this time. Instead of two log cabins there was only one.

I looked to see if Stackpoole was in place. She was, having climbed onto a table that had been set up behind the cabin flat. Though the table legs wobbled, she managed to stay steady and climb up on the stool. That allowed her to look over the roof of the cabin.

"Go!" I whispered to Saltz.

"Can't!" he whispered back just as fiercely.

"Now what?"

"Supposed to be a light . . ."

"Pass this to Stackpoole," I said, giving the flashlight to Root, one of the stagehands. "I'll get . . ." I was about to tell him I was going to lower the curtain, but he didn't wait. In full view of the audience he ran out on stage, handed the flashlight to Stackpoole, then raced back.

Round of applause for his effort.

Saltz hitched up his tights, adjusted his sword, slapped the tassel out of his face, and, bells jangling, marched onstage. Once there, he paused, obviously hesitant.

I made a quick check of the script to see what was supposed to be happening. I saw it. In a whisper I called, "Stackpoole, the light!"

Stackpoole turned on the flashlight.

Saltz started to act. He said: "Soft! What light through yonder window breaks?"

When she popped her head up, Saltz did this double take. Turning to the audience, he said: "She speaks!"

Stackpoole looked first one way, then another, and whispered: "O Romeo, Romeo! Wherefore art thou Romeo?"

From the back of the hall came a yell, "Louder!"

Stackpoole took a breath and repeated the words: "O Romeo, Romeo! Wherefore art thou Romeo?"

Saltz started to act again, trying to kneel before her. I say tried because he didn't make it. What happened was his feet, bells and all, got tangled up with his sword. Down he went, splat!—a headlong sprawl on his guts.

The audience thought it was funny.

Not knowing what to do, but trying to protect my pal, I leaped to the switch box and pulled. The curtain came crashing down.

Cheers from the audience.

"You okay?" I called to Saltz.

"Yeah," he called back, but not with a whole lot of energy.

I shot the curtain up again, revealing Saltz brushing himself off. When he realized the audience was watching him, he stopped his clean-up, then tried kneeling again. That time he made it, but only after he had flung his sword away in disgust.

Stackpoole decided to give her line a third time.

She said: "O Romeo, Romeo! Wherefore art thou Romeo?"

Saltz said: "Call me by love, and I will be new baptized; henceforth I won't be Romeo."

To which Stackpoole replied: "How come you hither, wherefore and why not?"

Saltz said: "With love's light winds did I buy these walls."

And Stackpoole: "If they do see thee, they will . . . will . . ."

She stopped; she had forgotten the next word. I grabbed my script again to see what it was supposed to be. Except I couldn't. She had my flashlight.

"Line, please," Stackpoole whispered.

I held the script high in the air, trying to get some stage light on it. I found the word. "Murder!" I shouted.

"Call the cops!" came a shout from someone in the audience.

Stackpoole said: ". . . murder thee."

Saltz:

"I have night's cloak to hide me from their eyes;
And but thou love me, let them find me here."

Stackpoole: "O, gentle Romeo, I just . . ."

Once more she stopped and looked offstage toward

me. My first thought was that she had forgotten her line again. But no, she repeated it: "O, gentle Romeo, I just . . ."

My mistake. I was supposed to make a noise. I stamped my feet.

She went on: "I just heard some noise. Dear love, a dew."

Saltz put his hand to his heart: "Good night, good night. Sweety is such a party . . ."

Realizing he had it wrong he tried again: "Such a sweet party . . ."

And again: "Parting is such sweet and sour that tomorrow I shall say good night till it be sorry."

I flipped all the switches. The lights went on full blast, not off.

27

♡ ♡

SALTZ CAME offstage, his face ghastly white. "I messed up my lines," he informed me.

I didn't care. "Get back on!" I yelled at him. "Hays! You're on."

Saltz went back, and in a moment Hays, playing Friar Lawrence, a priest, joined him.

Hays had a costume that consisted of a plaid bathrobe tied around his middle with a rope. A lady's swim cap was on his head, which I think was meant to make him look bald. Actually, the whole outfit made him look like he was about to enter the 400-meter dog paddle.

The two stood there side by side, facing the audience.

Hays said: "Where hast thou been?"
Saltz:
"Plainly know my heart's dear love is set
On the fair daughter of rich Capulet.

I pray that thou consent to marry us today."

Hays looked at him and said: "Wisely and slow; they stumble that run fast."

Saltz nodded, then to prove Hays's point, he stumbled offstage, though I didn't think he meant to do it. Hays followed. No sooner did Saltz come off than he went back on. Priscilla was with him.

Saltz: "Nurse, commend me to thy lady."

Priscilla: "I will tell her as much."

Saltz: "Bid her devise some means to come to church this afternoon. And there, at Friar Lawrence's cell we'll be shaved and married."

So saying, Saltz turned about, snappy as a soldier, and marched off—leaving Priscilla. She was looking right at me. I didn't know why. She mouthed some words. I didn't get it. Finally, she made a beckoning gesture.

I went to the edge of the side curtain. "What?" I whispered.

"Juliet," she whispered back. "Supposed to be here."

Just then, Stackpoole, holding her dress to keep from tripping, rushed up, her face red with embarrassment. Not stopping, she ran onto the stage. Breathless, she said: "Did you meet with him?"

Priscilla: "Go you to Friar Lawrence's cell. There stays a husband to make you a wife."

The two of them turned and walked off, bumping

into Hays who was returning. The bump caused his bathing cap to inch up, making the dome of his head look like a huge, swelling zit. Unaware, he said: "So smile the heavens upon this holy act."

He held out his hands to either side, and looked expectantly first toward one wing, then the other. No one showed.

"You're supposed to come back," he whispered out loud.

Saltz came back.

Hays turned to the other side. "You too," he urged.

Stackpoole, looking flustered, also returned.

Hays took their hands and said: "We will make short work; by your leaves, you shall not stay alone till Holy Church makes two equal one."

With those words he gave a big nod, which made his bathing cap shoot up and off, revealing his mohawk haircut. With a smart grab he caught the cap, and they all walked off.

End of act two. I never felt so exhausted in my life.

28

"WHAT TIME is it?" I asked nobody in particular.

"Past four" was the answer.

We were supposed to have finished five minutes ago.

"You want to give up?" Hamilton suggested.

"No way," I said, and gripping my flashlight, I turned to the switches.

The cast got ready to move on stage.

"Hold it!" came a cry. "Sondstrom is missing."

At that moment Sondstrom rushed on, buttoning his costume. He had been in the boys' room.

Saltz, pulling up his tights, led his gang onstage.

The ice-covered log cabins were back in place. Still, the characters made a show of wiping sweat from their faces. As they did, Hamilton entered with his gang from the other side of the stage. They looked as though they had just escaped from a pro wrestling costume camp, all decked out in science fiction uniforms. One had a space helmet under his arm.

Hamilton pointed to Saltz and said: "Romeo, the hate I bear thee can afford no better term than this: thou art a villain!"

Saltz remembered that he was supposed to start walking off, which he did. What he didn't remember was that he had a line to say first. So, back he went and said: "Farewell!"

Hamilton jumped forward and yanked his broken sword out of his belt. His pals did the same. Hamilton said:

"Boy, this shall not excuse the injuries

That thou hast done me; therefore turn and draw!"

Saltz and his team drew their swords. That would have been fine, except Saltz had thrown his away during the last act, and had forgotten to get it back. Radosh came to his rescue. He snapped his in two and gave half to Saltz. True, their swords looked more like blunt daggers than swords, but it was something.

Meanwhile, as soon as the audience realized there was going to be a fight, they began to howl with glee. Hamilton couldn't resist. He made a big bow to the audience, while his friends lifted their fingers, sports fashion, to claim that they were "Number One."

The fight began. It consisted of everybody holding swords out as far as they could and waving and whacking them.

Except, once again, Hamilton had to do things his way. He began to dance around, darting in and out, poking his sword at Saltz from all sides, but mostly from the rear.

People in the audience started to laugh.

Saltz got mad. He tried to fight back. His sword being what it was, that wasn't easy. Then he stepped on one of his long slippers, tripped and went down on the stage with a thump.

Quickly, Hamilton put a foot on Saltz's backside and lifted his arms in triumph.

The audience hooted, whistled, and stomped.

Actually, what should have happened was that Mercutio, a friend of Romeo's, was supposed to be killed. But that character, played by Gullette, was still standing, untouched. Ignored. All the same, he called out: "I am hurt! A plague a both your houses! I'm speeding. They've made worm meat of me."

He went down with a crash. The whole stage shook. Icicles fell. So did a log cabin.

In the bedlam Saltz got out from under Hamilton's foot. Furious, his face burning, he flung away his sword and dove at Hamilton—a full tackle. Down they went, pounding each other in full view of everyone. It was for real.

The audience, thinking it all part of the show, screamed with delight.

Now the other people on the stage joined the fight. They weren't kidding either. I mean, even the supposedly dead Mercutio got up and jumped in.

It was too much. I got the curtain to crash down

and cut the lights. The audience was on its feet, whistling, calling for more.

I ran from the wings. "Cut it out!" I yelled, "Stop it!" as I dragged people apart. "Take your places," I said and dove backstage before they could start fighting again.

By the time the curtain went up again, things looked different. Mercutio was back on the ground acting dead, as he was meant to be. Hamilton was also down. He too was supposed to be dead (killed by Romeo), but he had his eyes wide open and was breathing furiously. In the middle of it all stood Saltz, breathing just as hard, costume ripped and cockeyed. Somehow, he managed to say: "O, I am fortune's fool," and ran off stage.

After a moment, when nobody did anything, Porter went onstage. He was the Prince of Verona. You could tell he was in charge because he wore a paper crown (from Burger King) and carried a scepter. He took a look at all the bodies and asked the audience: "Where are the pile of beginners who began this fray?"

He put a finger to his head like a cartoon character thinking, then held it up in the air as if he had managed to get an idea from somewhere.

He said: "Romeo slew him. He slew Mercutio. We do exile Romeo."

At that point, instead of waiting for the curtain

to drop, all of the dead people on stage got up and walked off.

"Rematch!" suggested someone from the audience.

I peeked out front. Mr. Sullivan had stood up and was heading to where Mrs. Bacon was sitting.

I cut the lights, thinking that Sullivan was about to cut the show.

But I hoped not. The first kissing scene was coming up.

29

♡ ♡

SALTZ CAME over fuming and breathing hard. "Did you see what Hamilton did?" he demanded.

"Forget it," I told him. "He won't be on the stage anymore."

"Fat chance."

"Hey," I said, "put your mind to the bedroom scene. It's soon."

Even in the dark I saw the blood drain from his face. Without another word he wandered off.

Hearing nothing from Sullivan—as far as I could see he had gone back to his seat—I got the curtain up and the blue lights on. Betsy on spotlight started to look for Stackpoole and after a few bad guesses found her.

She was alone on the stage, kneeling, looking awfully small in that huge costume. The blue lights, right for once, gave an eerie look. Strands of hair hung over her face. Nervously, she brushed them away and looked up. Her eyes were bright, her freckled face frightened. Slowly, she placed her hands together as if praying. She spoke softly to the silence:

"Give me my Romeo; and when he shall die,
Take him and cut him out in little stars,
And he will make the face of heaven so fine
That all the world will be in love with night
And pay no worship to the garish sun."

When she finished speaking, she gave a little sigh. The sigh floated out over the audience and for once held it still. I felt a shiver zip up my spine. Saltz was right; Stackpoole was something special.

The mood lasted only a few seconds. Priscilla went onstage. Stackpoole pushed herself up onto her feet and said: "Now, Nurse, what news? Why do you wring your hands?"

Priscilla did a curtsy, adjusted her cap when it almost came off, and answered: "Tybalt is gone and Romeo killed him. He is banished. Shame come to Romeo!"

Stackpoole replied: "Shall I speak ill of him that is my husband? Give this ring to my true knight, and bid him come to take his last farewell."

Then Stackpoole gave a pull to the ring. It wouldn't come off. She pulled again.

From the audience came the call, "Harder!" Others joined in.

Stackpoole tried to take their advice. It didn't work. Priscilla tried. It still wouldn't give.

It was then that Stackpoole was heard to say, "Oh . . . darn!" and both she and Priscilla walked off the stage to a lot of applause.

From the other side, Hays, still in his bathrobe, his bathing cap firmly back in place, came on. Saltz was with him.

Saltz: "Father, what news?"

Hays: "From Verona art thou banished."

Saltz: " 'Tis torture, and not mercy; heaven is where Juliet lives."

Priscilla came running onto the stage, and said: "I come from Lady Juliet. Here is a ring, sir, that she bade me give you."

She held out her hand. It was obvious to anyone who looked that nothing was there. At first Saltz seemed puzzled. But when Priscilla kept offering nothing, he caught on. He pretended to take the ring, only to forget it the next moment.

He said: "I were a brief so brief to part with fare well."

I cut the lights, brought down the curtain. "Get the set ready!" I called. The stagehands rushed out and set things up.

I looked to see if the stage was ready. Stackpoole was standing on a stool that had been placed on that wobbly table so she could lean over the one remaining flat. Even at that she had to stretch.

In front of the log cabin was another table. Saltz

lumbered out and climbed onto it. There they were, what the whole thing was about: the kissing scene. Would they or wouldn't they?

I wasn't the only one watching. The entire class was standing in the wings, both sides, waiting to see what would happen.

Still, something didn't seem right.

Remembering all on my own, I ran back, hoisted the curtain, and switched on the lights.

They began. . . .

Saltz, his arms spread wide, said: "Farewell, farewell; one kiss, and I'll descend."

From the audience there were helpful shouts of encouragement, cheers, catcalls, and whistles, including a few "Go for it" remarks.

Saltz blotched red. Sweat glistened. But there he was, stretching upward, his mouth puckered just as I told him to. He must have practiced on the Cabbage Patch Kid.

For her part, Stackpoole was leaning down over the log cabin flat, equally red faced, equally puckered, unable to see much because of her hair. Try as hard as they did, they still couldn't quite meet.

"Closer!" came a cry. I'll always believe it was Hamilton.

Saltz strained. Stackpoole strained. I held my breath. I don't know who, but one of them lost his balance. Down came the log cabin flat. Down went

Saltz. Down went Stackpoole. Down went assorted furniture.

Saltz was on the bottom. On top, in order, was a table, a flat, a girl pretending to be Juliet, another table, a stool. A near riot in the audience.

I rushed onstage, pulling all that stuff—including Stackpoole—away. She was unhurt, but then she was close to the top.

When I got down to Saltz, I found him with his eyes closed.

"Saltz! I called. "You okay?"

His eyes fluttered open.

"You okay?" I demanded.

Saltz sat up slowly. He gave his head a shake.

"Say something," I pleaded.

And he did speak. He said, "That was some kiss."

30

"LIGHTS, PLEASE!" came the voice of Mr. Sullivan. "I want the lights." I left Saltz and got some lights on, which I managed only after a few mistakes.

When I looked out into the assembly hall, I saw Sullivan standing down front. "I want the entire cast on stage," he ordered. People, not knowing whether to laugh or cry (some were doing both), gathered. Saltz, still woozy, remained sitting on the floor.

I noticed Mrs. Bacon in one of the back row seats. She had a handkerchief over her face. I don't know if she was hiding or not wanting to see.

Sullivan looked us over and scowled. Then he turned to the audience, which had grown very quiet.

"I want your complete attention," he said, trying to squash the last bits of restlessness. Teachers were prowling the aisles.

"We have already gone way beyond our allotted time," Mr. Sullivan continued, looking very serious. "If you people (in the audience) can't keep yourselves under control, we're going to end it right here."

A few moans. A couple of hisses.

"Is that understood?" Sullivan demanded. There was no answer. He turned to us, waiting nervously.

"Is Peter all right?" he asked.

Saltz's voice: "Fine."

"Ed," Sullivan continued, "are you going to be able to finish this thing in good order?"

"It was finished before we began," I heard Hamilton say but not so loud that Sullivan caught it.

I looked around at my classmates for an answer. They were nodding.

"I think we can finish it," I told Sullivan.

He turned back to the audience. "Okay," he said. "We will proceed. But . . . if there are more disturbances, *any more*, I'll end it right there. Understood? Understood," he echoed, sure of the agreement he had just made with himself.

As he marched back to his seat, there was a burst of applause. It wasn't for Sullivan. I knew that. They were having a good time with us.

"Okay, people," I said to the class. "Let's go."

In moments the stage was clear. I took my place by the lights. Saltz was standing there, a slightly dazed look still on his face.

"You going to make it?" I asked.

"What a kiss," he murmured. "What a kiss!"

I reached for the switches and made everything dark. It occurred to me that it might be safer that way.

31

♡ ♡

STACKPOOLE was on stage, her dress torn and only half the length it had been when she began. Standing next to her was Hays, his mohawk exposed once again. He said: "Tomorrow night look that you lie alone; take thou this vial . . . ."

From under his robe he produced a soda bottle with a cork shoved into it. He went on: "This liquor drink off. Presently, through all your veins shall run a cold and drowsy humor. No warmth, no breath, shall testify you are alive. You'll sleep for two and forty hours and then awake from a pleasant sleep. Romeo by my letters will know what you've done and hither shall he come. That night he'll take you up to Mantua."

Stackpoole took the soda bottle, looked at it and said: "Lord give me strength."

The two of them walked off, but the next moment Stackpoole came back alone, holding the bottle. She held it out and faced the audience, saying:

"My dismal scene I needs must act alone.

Come, vial.

What if it be a poison . . .

Romeo, I come! This do I drink to thee."

She pulled at the cork. It wouldn't come. First the ring, now the cork. She had strength of character but not much strength of strength.

She gave it another try. Still it wouldn't come. She looked off into the wings. I shook my head, not knowing what to do. "Try it again," I whispered.

What she did was turn her back to the audience and try, with the bottle clamped between her knees, to get that cork out. Wouldn't budge. She tried her teeth. Still no luck.

Again she faced the wings. "I can't do it," she said very plainly.

The audience was working hard at controlling itself.

Figuring that we couldn't get the play going forward unless she drank the stuff, I walked onstage.

A few claps.

Stackpoole handed me the bottle, and I gave it a try. In fact, I tried a couple of times, really straining. I couldn't get it out either. When I looked up, Saltz was standing next to me.

"Here," he said. "I'll hold the bottle. You pull the cork."

Which is what we did. A real tug of war. But it worked. We got the cork out.

The audience gave up trying to control itself and cheered.

I handed the bottle back to Stackpoole, then Saltz and I walked offstage.

Alone again, Stackpoole studied the bottle and repeated her lines: "My dismal scene I must needs act alone. Come, vial. What if it be a poison . . . Romeo! I drink to thee."

With that, she lifted the bottle high, pretending to pour whatever was in there into her mouth. Maybe she thought it was empty.

It wasn't. The poison—grape juice, I think—gushed out. Very little went into her mouth, though, and what did made her collapse into a coughing fit, gagging and spewing what she took in. Most of the rest poured down over her dress, and onto the floor.

Biggest roar of laughter yet.

Disgusted, Stackpoole dropped the bottle and collapsed into a heap, right into the puddle, and acted unconscious, which was probably what she wanted to be.

I looked around. Priscilla was supposed to go on. "Priscilla?" I called.

Priscilla had been watching so hard she missed her cue. Now, to make up for lost time, she ran on, right into the puddle, right over the bottle. She could have been on roller skates the way she moved. Her feet went one way, the rest another. With a crash she came down.

I'm not going to tell you what the audience did.

Priscilla got up on her hands and knees. Dripping grape juice, she looked at Stackpoole. Then, like a good nurse, she used the stethoscope to see if Juliet was showing any signs of life.

Finally, she looked at the audience and said: "O lemon table day!"

Then it was the turn of Juliet's mother to get on stage, the part supposed to be played by Amy Jefferson. Except Amy was sick, and I was to have found someone else to play the part for her. Only I never had.

There wasn't much choice. *I* ran out on stage, script in hand. What's more, I ran right into the slosh. I went down too, then sat up, searched through the script (which I had managed to hold onto) and said: "What is the matter?"

After the audience stopped their hysterics, Priscilla replied: "Look, O heavy day!"

I read: "O me, O me, my child, my only life! Help!"

Priscilla said: "She's dead, deceased; she's dead, I lack a day."

I added: "I lack a day too. She's dead."

Now it was time for Hays to appear. He came on and fortunately managed to avoid the puddle. He looked at Stackpoole, and said: "Everyone prepare to follow this fair corpse into her grave."

It was Priscilla and me, wet and dripping, who picked up Stackpoole, also wet and dripping, and carried her offstage. Hays watched us go, trying to keep from laughing.

I told someone to get a mop. In reply someone told me that Hamilton had disappeared. For me that was a bright spot.

32

ALL I WANTED was to get the thing done. What's more, from the looks of the people around me, I think there was general agreement about that. Except for Saltz. I didn't know what was going on in his head. But from the dreamy look on his face I was beginning to think that crash had truly knocked him silly. He was acting as if he was actually enjoying the performance.

And Stackpoole . . . She was soaking wet and shivering from her external dose of poison.

Priscilla, who was acting the Nurse to the hilt, was trying to dry Stackpoole off.

"She can't go on," she whispered fiercely.

"She has to if we're going to finish," I said.

"She needs another costume."

"Fine," I agreed. "Where's Jessie?" At that point we were running half an hour overtime. And there were increasing numbers of hoots and whistles from out front.

Jessie appeared. I'm not sure, but I think she was wearing that old King Kong costume from the costume room.

"New costume for Stackpoole!" I begged, and she, with a bunch of others, whisked Stackpoole away for a change. She had about one minute.

"You're on," I told Saltz.

He gave a hitch to his tights and lumped across the stage. He was met by DuBois, coming from the other side.

Saltz said: "How now, Balthasar! How fares my Juliet? For nothing wells ill if she be canned."

DuBois returned: "Her body sleeps in the Capulet monument, and her immortal part with the angels lives."

To this sad news Saltz put on a tremendous show of acting. Stretching his arms wide, he groaned, then clapped his hand to his head and gave another moan. It might have looked good except that under all that pressure his jacket, too small from the start, split in two. All the same, he said: "Hire post-horses. I will hence tonight."

Off they ran in opposite directions, Saltz getting rid of his busted jacket once offstage.

"Stackpoole's ready," Jessie said to me.

I got the curtain down so that people could put out a table that had a cloth draped over it reaching down to the floor. It was supposed to be the tomb of the Capulets.

I switched the lights to murk.

"Stackpoole's supposed to be out there," I said.

I peered across the stage. Sure enough, I saw what I took to be her running across the stage; then someone else gave her a hand up onto the table. I turned to look for Saltz.

"Right here," he said and brushed past me onto the stage. Only then did I see what he had on underneath that torn jacket. It was his Born in the USA T-shirt. He'd also been trying to keep up his tights with a pair of rainbow-colored suspenders.

Onstage again, Saltz stopped walking and started acting. I guess he couldn't do both at once. Seeing Stackpoole on the table, he went up to her. I got the lights brighter.

Saltz said: "Ah, dear Juliet. Why are thou yet so fair? Eyes, look your last! Here's to my love!"

He pulled out the same soda bottle/poison that Stackpoole had used. Fortunately, he didn't have to worry about a cork. It was empty. Lifting the bottle, he said: "The drugs are quick." He did the drinking bit, flung the bottle away (it shattered, I'm afraid), and approached the table.

"Thus with a kiss I die."

The *second* kissing scene.

Once more people had gathered in the wings to watch.

Saltz was close to the table, near to Stackpoole. He bent over. Closer . . . closer.

A bright flash! An explosion! Saltz leaped back. Stackpoole jumped up. Smoke billowed out from underneath the table, filling the stage with murky stink. People in the audience came to their feet. Some shouted. A couple screamed. Mostly, though, people were stunned, not knowing what to think.

Then, out from under the table, out from the cloud of smoke, crawled Hamilton, his face whiter than the smoke except for smudges of soot. One hand held the other as if he were in pain. A tear ran down his cheek.

I never saw anyone move as fast as Sullivan did. Somehow he managed to get to Hamilton first.

"I didn't mean to do that," I heard Hamilton stammer. (Sure, he just happened to be under the table with a firecracker and matches.) He really looked ghastly, scared out of the few wits he had.

Sullivan—keeping one hand on Hamilton's shoulder—stood up and looked about, first at the cast, then at the audience. He was making up his mind.

"You almost done?" he said to me.

All I could do was nod.

"I think it would be best to finish up," he said. "Albert, you come with me." He helped Hamilton up and led him off. The guy, obviously hurting and scared, slumped as he walked away. I almost felt sorry for him.

"Where were we?" I asked nobody in particular.

"Romeo was kissing Juliet," Hays offered.

They waited for my decision.

"Forget it," I said. "Too dangerous."

The audience settled back. Stackpoole climbed onto the table again. Saltz sat down and leaned against the table, dead.

It was time for Hays to rush back on. He said: "Romeo! O, pale! Ah, what unkind hour is guilty of this lemon table chance!"

Stackpoole, hearing this, sat up like a jack-in-the-box and cried: "Where is my Romeo?"

To which Hays replied: "Thy husband there lies dead."

Stackpoole crawled to the edge of the table and looked down at Saltz, propped up against a table leg so everybody could read his Born in the USA T-shirt. Peering down at him, Stackpoole said: "Poison, I see, hath been his timeless end."

Then she stood up, holding a rubber dagger high over her head. Only then did I see what Jessie had found to replace the white dress: a Statue of Liberty costume. I guess it went with Saltz's T-shirt. Oh, they did go together!

Stackpoole said: "O happy dagger! This is my sheath! There rust and let me die."

With that she shoved the knife at her middle. The blade, being rubber, bent like a pretzel. She flopped down anyway. As she did, a hail of paper airplanes—

118

made from the play programs—flew over the stage, a final gift from the audience.

Hays stepped forward toward the audience and said:

"For never was a story of more woe

Than this of Juliet and her Romeo."

At that point Saltz and Stackpoole both got up, just as everybody else from the production poured onstage to take a bow.

People actually clapped.

Probably because it was over.

33

IT WAS OVER. It was done. Aside from the fact that we were glad, we were exhausted.

Still, some things had been accomplished.

Right after the production Betsy Hays appeared out of nowhere.

"Did I do okay?" she asked.

I was so happy to be done with it all that I flung my arms around her in a big hug. "You were great!" I told her.

Startled, she backed off, looked at me, blushed, then ran away.

Next morning Hays told me his sister thought that not only was I a theater genius, I was the nicest boy in the world. "Just no more bright ideas, okay?" he urged.

Hamilton spent two days in the hospital with a badly burned hand, plus one week home (suspended) for being a jerk.

Both Saltz and Stackpoole were smash hits. Stars. Everyone told them how great they were.

As for Saltz *and* Stackpoole, all I can say is that when I got to class the next morning, the two of them were sitting side by side. She was reading a book called *Great Tragic Actresses of All Time*.

He was busy writing away—a poem, I'm sure. Maybe a play. I never saw it. He gave it to her.

The most interesting result, for me, came the night after the production. It was a phone call from Lucy.

"Ed?"

"Yes."

"This is Lucy."

"Oh, hi."

"That was really great, wasn't it?"

"I guess," I admitted.

"Know what I just found out?"

"What?"

"Next term we read another Shakespeare play."

My heart sank. "No kidding," I said.

"It's all about Cleopatra."

"Oh."

"And I was thinking . . . you know . . . if we wanted to, we could put on that play, too. Only I'd like to be Cleopatra."

"Well, you see . . ."

"And in the play—this is what someone told me—

she has a boyfriend. Anthony. What I thought is, you could play that part. What do you think?"

In a flash, that definition of love from the dictionary went through my mind. All those things you had to do! It was almost as hard as putting on a play. So I said, "I don't know. Probably too much work."

"Well, think about it," she said. "See you tomorrow."

After she hung up, I sat there for a while. Then— just curious—I went to a book of Shakespeare my folks had and read *Antony and Cleopatra.*

Wasn't half bad.